To: Katherine
From: Elyss

D0361493

# Karen's Kite

**Look for these
and other books about Karen
in the
Baby-sitters Little Sister series:**

# 1 Karen's Witch
# 2 Karen's Roller Skates
# 3 Karen's Worst Day
# 4 Karen's Kittycat Club
# 5 Karen's School Picture
# 6 Karen's Little Sister
# 7 Karen's Birthday
# 8 Karen's Haircut
# 9 Karen's Sleepover
#10 Karen's Grandmothers
#11 Karen's Prize
#12 Karen's Ghost
#13 Karen's Surprise
#14 Karen's New Year
#15 Karen's in Love
#16 Karen's Goldfish
#17 Karen's Brothers
#18 Karen's Home Run
#19 Karen's Good-bye
#20 Karen's Carnival
#21 Karen's New Teacher
#22 Karen's Little Witch
#23 Karen's Doll
#24 Karen's School Trip
#25 Karen's Pen Pal
#26 Karen's Ducklings
#27 Karen's Big Joke
#28 Karen's Tea Party
#29 Karen's Cartwheel

#30 Karen's Kittens
#31 Karen's Bully
#32 Karen's Pumpkin Patch
#33 Karen's Secret
#34 Karen's Snow Day
#35 Karen's Doll Hospital
#36 Karen's New Friend
#37 Karen's Tuba
#38 Karen's Big Lie
#39 Karen's Wedding
#40 Karen's Newspaper
#41 Karen's School
#42 Karen's Pizza Party
#43 Karen's Toothache
#44 Karen's Big Weekend
#45 Karen's Twin
#46 Karen's Baby-sitter
#47 Karen's Kite
#48 Karen's Two Families

Super Specials:
# 1 Karen's Wish
# 2 Karen's Plane Trip
# 3 Karen's Mystery
# 4 Karen, Hannie, and
      Nancy: The Three
      Musketeers
# 5 Karen's Baby
# 6 Karen's Campout

## Little Sister

# Karen's Kite

### Ann M. Martin

Illustrations by Susan Tang

A
**LITTLE APPLE**
PAPERBACK

SCHOLASTIC INC.
New York Toronto London Auckland Sydney

*If you purchased this book without a cover, you should be aware that this book is stolen property. It was reported as "unsold and destroyed" to the publisher, and neither the author nor the publisher has received any payment for this "stripped book."*

No part of this publication may be reproduced in whole or in part, or stored in a retrieval system, or transmitted in any form or by any means, electronic, mechanical, photocopying, recording, or otherwise, without written permission of the publisher. For information regarding permission, write to Scholastic Inc., 555 Broadway, New York, NY 10012.

ISBN 0-590-46913-4

Copyright © 1994 by Ann M. Martin. All rights reserved. Published by Scholastic Inc. APPLE PAPERBACKS ® and BABY-SITTERS LITTLE SISTER ® are registered trademarks of Scholastic Inc.

12 11 10 9 8 7 6 5 4 3                    4 5 6 7 8/9

Printed in the U.S.A.                    40

First Scholastic printing, March 1994

*The author gratefully acknowledges*
*Stephanie Calmenson*
*for her help*
*with this book.*

# Karen's Kite

# Flying

"'Bye, Mommy! 'Bye, Andrew!" I called.

I jumped out of Mommy's car and raced into my second grade class at Stoneybrook Academy.

I love school. I am in the same class as my two best friends, Nancy Dawes and Hannie Papadakis. We do almost everything together. That is why we call ourselves the Three Musketeers.

My teacher's name is Ms. Colman. She is gigundoly smart. She always can understand and explains things...

them. And she hardly ever raises her voice, even when I forget and raise mine. (I do that a lot.) Then she just says, "Indoor voice, please, Karen."

That is my name. Karen. My whole name is Karen Brewer. I am seven years old. I have blonde hair, blue eyes, and some freckles. I wear glasses, too. The blue pair is for reading and the pink pair is for all the other times I need glasses. (I do not need them when I am sleeping or in the bathtub.)

Two other kids in my class wear glasses. They are Ricky Torres (he is my pretend husband), and Natalie Springer. We sit together in the front row. Ms. Colman says we can see better from there. (She wears glasses herself.)

Ms. Colman was writing on the black-
b... so I went straight to my seat. On
the ...
(They ... I waved to Hannie and Nancy.
because ti-ther at the back of the room
Ms. Colma... not wear glasses.)
tion. It was: ...riting a Mystery Ques-

*What do these six things have in common?*

This was a gigundoly good mystery.

"While I am taking attendance, please think about the question on the blackboard," said Ms. Colman.

Ms. Colman called my name first.

"Here!" I answered. Then I started thinking. I could tell the other kids were thinking too.

Addie Sidney was tapping her pencil on the tray of her wheelchair. Pamela Harding was tapping her chin with her finger. (Pamela is my best enemy.) Jannie Gilbert and Leslie Morris, Pamela's friends, were pointing at the blackboard and whispering. T and Tammy Barkan, the twins, were writing notes to each other. Bobby Gianelli tried to grab the twins' note. (Bobby is a sometimes bully.)

Hank Reubens raised his hand. Then he changed his mind and put it back down. Good. I wanted to get the answer first.

"Wheep-wheep!" called Hootie. He is our class guinea pig. Maybe he had the answer. He is very smart — for a guinea pig.

Just then, I saw a bird fly by the window. A picture of a bird was on the blackboard. Birds fly. So do airplanes. And bats. And kites. And . . .

I waved my hand so hard it almost flew off my arm.

"Yes, Karen?" said Ms. Colman.

"I solved the mystery! They are all things that can fly!" I cried.

"Good for you, Karen," said Ms. Colman, smiling.

I grinned. I had figured out the answer first. (Well, maybe Hootie knew the answer. But Ms. Colman called on me.)

"Today we will begin learning about flight," said Ms. Colman. "We are going to study living and mechanical things that can fly and how they do it. We will even go on a field trip to our local airport."

Yes! A class trip to the airport. I told you I love school!

# Weekends

Mommy and Andrew were waiting for me after school.

"Guess what! Guess what!" I cried. "Ms. Colman is taking our class on a trip to the airport!"

"That's exciting news," said Mommy.

"Will you get to fly in an airplane?" asked Andrew.

"No. But we will probably go inside one," I replied.

Andrew is my little brother. He is four going on five. I will tell you something interesting about Andrew and me. We have two houses and two families. Here is how that happened.

A long time ago, Mommy and Daddy were married. But when Andrew and I were very little, Mommy and Daddy started fighting a lot. They loved Andrew and me, but they were so unhappy with each other that they did not want to be married anymore. So they got divorced.

After the divorce, Daddy stayed in our big house in Stoneybrook. (He grew up there.) Mommy moved with Andrew and me to a little house not too far away. That is where Andrew and I live most of the time.

Then Mommy and Daddy each got married again to other people. Mommy married Seth Engle. Now he is my stepfather. He moved into the little house with his cat, Rocky, and his dog, Midgie. So we all live in the little house together. Oh, yes. My pet rat, Emily Junior, lives at the little house, too.

Daddy married Elizabeth Thomas. Now

she is my stepmother. She was married once before. She moved into the big house with her four children. They are Kristy, who is thirteen and the best stepsister ever, David Michael, who is seven, and Sam and Charlie, who are so old they're in high school.

Then Daddy and Elizabeth adopted Emily Michelle from a faraway country called Vietnam. She is two and a half. (I named my rat after her.) Nannie, who is Elizabeth's mother, moved in to help take care of her.

There are also pets at the big house: Shannon is a dog, Boo-Boo is a cat, and Crystal Light the Second and Goldfishie are elephants. (Just kidding. They are fish.)

Andrew and I live at the big house every other weekend and on some vacations and holidays. To make going back and forth easier, we have two of lots of different things. I have two bicycles, one at each house. Andrew has two tricycles. We have two sets of clothes and toys. I have two stuffed cats,

Goosie and Moosie. Goosie stays at the little house and Moosie stays at the big house. You already know that I have two best friends. Nancy lives next door to the little house and Hannie lives near the big house. I even have two pieces of Tickly, my special blanket.

Because Andrew and I have two of so many different things, I gave us a special name. I call us two-two's. (I thought of the name after Ms. Colman read our class a book called *Jacob Two-Two Meets the Hooded Fang*.)

Now, if only we had two airplanes. We could fly back and forth between our two houses whenever we wanted to. I think I'll talk to Mommy and Daddy about that tonight. (Just kidding again!)

# Sassy

On Wednesday morning, Ms. Colman made a Surprising Announcement. (Those are my favorite kind.)

"Class, we are going to have two special guests this morning. As soon as they arrive, I will ask Hank to introduce them."

As soon as Ms. Colman had finished taking attendance, a tall man walked into our room carrying a covered cage.

"This is my father," said Hank. Then Hank uncovered the cage. "And this is Sassy. He's my pet canary."

"Ooh, he's pretty!" I cried.

Sassy was bright yellow. He was sitting on his perch, turning his head from side to side.

"Why don't you come to the front of the room for a closer look," said Mr. Reubens.

Everyone gathered around the cage. Except for Natalie. She hung back. I think she was afraid. Natalie is afraid of a lot of things.

I could tell Sassy was happy to see us. He started to sing. Then he stopped singing and pecked at his feathers.

"What Sassy is doing now is called preening. That means he is cleaning his feathers," said Ms. Colman. "All birds have feathers. They are the only animals that have them. And all birds have wings. Most birds, though not all of them, can fly."

"If someone will close the door to the classroom for us, we can let Sassy out of his cage," said Mr. Reubens.

"I'll do it! I'll do it!" I cried.

Home work:
pg 21 - 26
pg 17-18

Today is

While I was closing the door, Ms. Colman was checking the windows. We did not want Sassy to fly away.

"We're ready," said Ms. Colman.

Hank opened the cage and held his finger out next to Sassy. Sassy hopped onto Hank's finger and stayed there while Hank carried him out.

"Cool!" said Ricky. "Will he fly?"

"Yes, I think he will," said Mr. Reubens. "He is used to being around people. He is very comfortable with them."

In no time Sassy was flying around the room. The minute he took off, Natalie ducked and covered her head.

"It's okay," I whispered to her. "He won't hurt you."

"Watch Sassy's wings closely," said Ms. Colman.

"He's flapping them," said Addie.

"But now he is just holding them still," said Nancy.

"That's right," said Ms. Colman. "Sassy flaps, then he glides."

Sassy flew back and forth across the room. Then he landed on Mr. Reubens' shoulder. The visit was over. We thanked Mr. Reubens for coming.

After he left, Ms. Colman showed us a film about living things that fly. We saw birds, insects, and bats.

"Bats are the only mammals that can fly," said Ms. Colman.

I wished I could fly. I decided to close my eyes and make believe. Now what should I be? Should I be a bat? No. I would have to eat insects for lunch. Should I be Sassy? No. I would have to live at Hank's house. What about a butterfly? Yes! I would be Karen, the Most Beautiful Butterfly.

But do butterflies wear glasses? Well, why not?

# Partners

Over the next few days, our class learned a lot about airplanes.

Ms. Colman told us that airplane wings work a lot like birds' wings. And we learned that the engine gives an airplane its power.

We made our own glider planes, too. (Gliders do not have engines.) We made some out of paper, and some out of wood.

"Now it is time to see some real airplanes," said Ms. Colman. "Remember that tomorrow is our trip to the airport. Karen,

I still do not have your permission slip. Please remember to bring it tomorrow. You can't go without it."

"I'll remember," I said.

The next morning, I walked into class waving my permission slip in the air. "I have my lunch money, too," I announced.

"I am glad you remembered, Karen," said Ms. Colman.

Three other grown-ups, aside from Ms. Colman, were going on the trip with us. There was Addie's mother, Bobby's grandmother, and Pamela's father. (Pamela was acting extra stuck-up because her father was coming on our trip.)

"It is time to choose partners," said Ms. Colman. "You and your partner will stick together the entire day."

"The entire day? The Three Musketeers *always* stick together!" I said.

Hannie, Nancy, and I held hands and walked to the front of the room in a line.

"I'm sorry, girls," said Ms. Colman. "I said partners, not teams."

Bullfrogs. But then Addie wheeled herself across the room to us.

"Do you want to be my partner, Nancy?" she asked.

"Great," said Nancy. "Karen and Hannie can be partners and we can *all* stick together."

The class was quickly pairing off. We were almost ready to go.

"Don't you have a partner, Natalie?" asked Ms. Colman. Natalie was standing by herself in a corner.

"There's nobody left," said Natalie in a teeny-tiny voice. (Natalie has a lisp. Sometimes she whispers so no one will hear it.)

"I'm puzzled," said Ms. Colman. "There are eighteen students in our class. That is an even number. Everyone should have a partner."

Ms. Colman looked around the room. In the back, Pamela, Jannie, and Leslie were holding hands.

"I would like one of you to be Natalie's

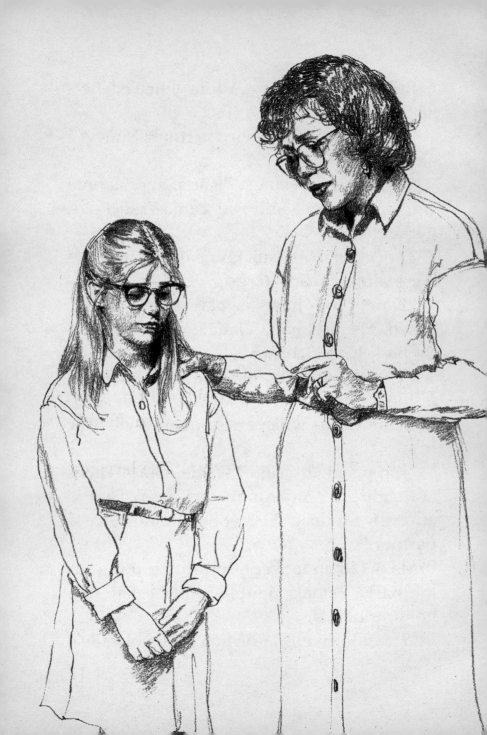

partner, please," said Ms. Colman.

Do you know what they did? They each took a step backward. I felt so, so bad for Natalie.

Ms. Colman said the girls were taking time away from our trip, and that one of them *had* to be partners with Natalie. So they drew straws. Leslie picked the short straw. (I was glad Pamela did not pick it. That would have been too bad for Natalie.)

Finally we got on the bus. Addie and Nancy had to sit in the back because of Addie's wheelchair. There were no seats left next to them. But Hannie and I had fun anyway. We pretended we were Lovely Ladies.

"Goodness, I hope we won't be late getting to the airport," said Hannie.

"Oh, no," I replied. "We would miss our flight to Paris. Our friends there would never forgive us."

All of a sudden we heard Leslie ask in a really loud voice, "Does anyone have a Baggie? I think Natalie is going to be bus sick."

Natalie's face looked kind of green. I grabbed a bag from my pack and passed it over. I hoped Natalie would not really get sick.

Poor, poor Natalie.

# The Airport

Luckily, Natalie made it through the half hour ride without getting sick. She started to look better as soon as we pulled into the airport parking lot.

"Hey, everyone! There's a plane taking off," said Bobby.

We piled out of the bus just in time to see it. It looked like a great big bird flying into the sky.

I liked this airport. It was not as big and crowded and noisy as the one I had been to before. (In case you did not know it, I flew on a plane once all by myself. I flew all the way to Nebraska to visit my granny and grandad.)

Inside the airport, a man was waiting to greet us.

"Welcome, everyone. I am Mr. King, the airport supervisor. First I will take you on a grand tour of one of our planes. Then we will visit the control tower."

Mr. King led us through the airport. Hannie and I held hands. So did Addie and Nancy.

Behind us Pamela, Jannie, and Leslie were holding hands, too. But no one was holding Natalie's hand. She was trailing along at the end of the line by herself.

I decided to keep an eye on her. Once I thought we lost her. But she had only bent down to pull up her socks. (Natalie's socks are always droopy.)

An empty plane was waiting for us in a corner of the runway. It was white with red and blue stripes.

We studied the wings, the wheels, the

tail, and the engines. Then we climbed up a stairway and went into the cockpit.

"Boy, look at all those knobs and buttons," I cried.

"These are the flight instruments. You use them to keep your plane on course," said Mr. King. He pointed out some of the instruments to us.

Then he said, "And these are the engine instruments. They let you know if your engine is working properly."

We each had a chance to be the pilot or copilot. We were not allowed to touch any buttons. But we could make believe. Hannie said I could be the pilot.

"Karen's Number One Jet coming in for a landing!" I announced. I made believe I was turning the control wheel.

"May Day! May Day!" called Hannie. "You just steered us into the airport cafeteria."

It was Leslie and Natalie's turn next. I could tell Leslie did not want Natalie to be her copilot.

"She will probably get airsick even though we are not moving," Leslie whispered to Pamela and Jannie.

I think Natalie heard her. She looked as if she might cry.

After everyone had taken a turn, we went to the control tower. We watched two planes take off and two planes land.

"Touchdown!" called Ricky when the planes' wheels hit the ground.

At noon it was time for lunch at the airport cafeteria. I thought it would be nice if the Three Musketeers and Addie could sit near Natalie. But Natalie took a long time deciding what to eat. By the time she was finished, no seats were left at our table.

I looked out of the cafeteria windows at the runway. I waved to a man who was boarding a plane.

Before we left, Mr. King introduced us to Ms. Lewis, a real live pilot. She gave each of us a pair of wings. When I got mine, I saluted. I was an official pilot.

# Kites

"We have learned about the flight of birds, bats, insects, and airplanes," said Ms. Colman on Friday. "Who can name something that flies without wings and without an engine?"

Everyone was stumped. Even me. Boy was I surprised when Natalie raised her hand. She only raised it a little bit. But Ms. Colman saw her.

"A Frisbee? Maybe?" said Natalie.

"The answer is a Frisbee for sure. That's very good, Natalie," said Ms. Colman.

"I have a Frisbee that glows in the dark," I added. (I forgot to raise my hand.)

Ms. Colman called on Terry next.

"How about a ball? It flies if you throw it," said Terry.

"You're right," said Ms. Colman. "Any other ideas? Yes, Audrey?"

"My cousin does not have wings or an engine. But he flew behind a boat once," said Audrey. "They attached him to a kite."

"Your cousin went parasailing, Audrey. The kite was called a parafoil. It can lift things as heavy as people," explained Ms. Colman. "I am glad you told us about your cousin. Today we are going to begin learning about kites and how they fly."

Oh, goody. I love kites. My favorites are the ones with bright colors and happy faces on them.

Ms. Colman told us lots of interesting things about kites. She told us that they were named after a very graceful bird called a kite. Every kite we fly has to have a line attached to it. There are hundreds of dif-

26

ferent kinds of kites. How they fly depends on how they are made.

While we were talking about kites, we heard a knock at the door. Mr. Mackey, our art teacher, poked his head in.

"Hello, everyone!" he said.

Mr. Mackey usually arrives with a cart of wonderful art supplies. Today he came with an armload of wonderful kites instead.

"Ms. Colman told me you were going to be learning about kites, so I brought some to show you," he said.

He had brought four different kinds. I had seen kites like them flying at Stoneybrook Playground. But I did not know they had important names. One was a flat kite. It is a kite that can be any shape, such as a square or a diamond. One was a box kite. It was shaped like a rectangle. One was a delta kite. It was shaped almost like a triangle. And one was the parafoil Ms. Colman had talked about. It was soft without too much shape of its own. It gets its shape from the wind.

"Soon each of you will have a chance to make a kite of your own," said Mr. Mackey. "And that is not all. We will hold a kite-flying contest when your kites are finished. You will get to stay after school on a Friday and fly your kites on the playground. Then we will have a school sleepover so we can watch the kites fly all night. Whoever builds the kite that stays up the longest wins the contest."

Everyone began talking and calling things out. Mr. Mackey held up his hand for quiet. He was not finished with his announcement yet.

"Before you begin making your kites, we will take a trip to Mrs. Moody's Kite Store. Mrs. Moody will tell us about the different kites she sells."

Mr. Mackey promised we would go on Wednesday. That was three school days away. I could hardly wait.

# Mrs. Moody

Saturday. Sunday. Monday. Tuesday. Wednesday! It was the day of our trip to Mrs. Moody's Kite Store.

Ms. Colman told us to team up with the same partners we had chosen for the trip to the airport.

"It's a short trip, and we do not want to waste any time," she explained.

That meant Leslie and Natalie were partners again. Leslie thought this was gigundoly unfair.

At nine-thirty, we piled onto the bus.

Addie's mother was there. Ricky's father came. And of course Ms. Colman and Mr. Mackey were there.

Hannie and I got to sit next to Addie and Nancy this time. We pretended we were four Lovely Ladies on our way to a tea party. But we could not play for very long. The ride to the store took only ten minutes.

Mrs. Moody was waiting for us at the door. She wore earrings shaped like kites. And she had a big smile. I liked her right away.

"Welcome, everyone. Please look around the store. Feel free to ask any questions you think of," she said.

I already had a question. I raised my hand. "Is it hard to make a kite?" I asked.

"Some kites are hard to make. But many others are easy. And they fly just as well," Mrs. Moody said.

I looked around. I was amazed. I saw so many kites. I saw cloth kites, paper kites, box kites. I saw kites shaped like monsters and animals. My two favorites were a

dragon and a tropical fish.

I thought of another question. But Hank was talking to Mrs. Moody. So I had to wait. Hank wanted to know if Mrs. Moody made kites herself.

"Yes, I do. I keep them at home. Sometimes I fly them. But mostly I just hang them up because they're pretty," she replied. "Karen, did you have another question?"

"Could you tell me if the dragon and the fish kites are very hard to make?" I asked.

"That dragon kite is a little complicated. But you could make a simple dragon kite. And the fish kite wouldn't be too hard."

"Oh, good," I said. "Those are my favorite ones."

"I have an announcement to make now, Karen," said Mrs. Moody. "I think you are going to like it."

"Hey, everyone. Mrs. Moody is going to make a Surprising Announcement!" I said.

That got everyone's attention.

"Thank you, Karen," said Mrs. Moody. She told us that she had heard about our kite-flying contest. "I would like to offer a prize to the winner," she said. "It is a twenty-five-dollar gift certificate to spend here in the store."

"Way cool!" said Hannie. "If I win, I am going to buy the butterfly kite."

"I will buy the caterpillar kite," said Nancy.

"I like the box kite," said Addie.

I found the price tags on the dragon and fish kites. They each cost thirty-one dollars and ninety-five cents. I decided I would make the fish kite at school. Then I could use the gift certificate to buy the dragon kite. I would just have to add a little bit of my own money.

But first I had to win the contest.

# Natalie's Bad News

It was a Sunday afternoon. Andrew and I were at the big house. We were waiting for Mommy to pick us up and take us back to the little house.

"Kai-kai," said Emily Michelle. She held up a piece of paper with colored squiggles on it. The squiggles were supposed to be kites. (*Kai-kai* was her word for kite.)

I had told everyone in my families that we were making kites at school. And I told them about our kite-flying contest and Mrs. Moody's prize.

"If I win, I am going to get a dragon kite!" I said.

*Honk! Honk!* Mommy had arrived.

" 'Bye, everyone!" we called. We raced to Mommy's car.

"Did you have a good weekend?" asked Mommy.

"Uh-huh," said Andrew. "We watched *The Little Mermaid* last night."

"Nannie helped us make popcorn. But guess who ate most of it," I said. "Shannon!" David Michael's puppy was a pig.

Andrew and I started singing songs from the movie. We were still singing when we walked into the little house.

Seth was on the phone. He put his finger to his lips. He was trying to tell us to please be quiet.

"Karen and her mother just walked in," he said into the phone. "I'll let them know what's going on."

"What is it?" I asked.

"Well, Karen, I'm afraid it is something a little sad. Natalie Springer's mother is on the phone. She is calling because Natalie's grandfather died suddenly. He was Mr. Springer's father," said Seth. "The Springers need to go to St. Louis to help Natalie's grandmother. Ordinarily, they would leave Natalie with her relatives. But the relatives will be going to St. Louis. So, since you and Natalie are in the same class, the Springers wondered if Natalie could stay here with us until they get back."

I was sorry to hear about Natalie's grandfather. It really was sad news.

"Of course Natalie can stay with us," said Mommy.

"Right," I agreed. Our families were not close friends. I wasn't even very good friends with Natalie. But this was very important. Natalie needed us.

Mommy got on the phone.

"Hello, Mrs. Springer," she said. "Natalie is welcome to stay with us as long as necessary. You can bring her over any time."

Mommy talked to Mrs. Springer a little

while longer. I could hear her making plans. Then she hung up the phone.

"The Springers will d̶r̶o̶p̶ ̶m̶e off on their way to the airport. They should be here around seven," said Mommy.

I drew in a deep breath. Our house is little, I thought. But it will just have to make room for one more person.

# Being Nice

I ran to my room to tell Goosie the news.

"We are going to have company, Goosie," I said. "You know Natalie Springer. She is in my class at school. She is the one who has droopy socks and — "

I heard a knock on my door. It was Mommy.

"May I talk with you for a minute, Karen?" she said.

"Okay," I replied.

Mommy sat on my bed.

"You know, Karen, Natalie will probably be upset. I do not know whether she was close to her grandfather. But even if she wasn't, this will be a difficult time for her," Mommy explained. "After all, her parents will be upset. And they will be leaving her and going far away. So I want you to be very nice to your guest."

I set Goosie down next to me and sat up on my bed. Taking care of Natalie while her parents were gone was going to be a very important job. A grown-up job.

"Don't worry, Mommy," I said. "I promise to be extra nice and helpful. I will let Natalie play with me all the time. She can have any of my toys. And I will never, ever fight with her."

"I know you'll try your best," said Mommy.

After our talk, I helped Mommy get sheets and towels ready for Natalie. I even put Hyacynthia, my special baby doll, on her bed for company.

After that, we ate dinner. Just as we were

finishing, the bell rang. Seth answered the door. The Springers stood together in a row. Natalie was in the middle.

I was amazed to see how much the Springers looked alike. They were *all* sloppy and droopy. *All* their socks were falling down. *All* their glasses were sliding down their noses. Natalie was just like her parents.

"Hi, Natalie. Come in," I said. "We are going to have fun together while you are here. I promise."

We visited in the living room until Natalie's parents had to leave. Then I took Natalie up to my room.

Mommy was right. Natalie really was upset. She was even crying a little bit.

"Hyacynthia is very good company. She can be your doll while you're here," I told her.

"Thanks, Karen," said Natalie.

"I am really sorry about your grandfather. Were you very good friends?" I asked.

"Not really. I didn't see him too much

because he lived so far away," said Natalie. "But now my parents are going to be far away, too. And I don't know when they will come back."

Natalie started crying again. I think she missed her parents already.

"Do you want to play a game? Or watch TV? Or I could read you a story, Natalie. I have some very funny books. They will cheer you up," I said.

I decided to do whatever Natalie wanted. She was feeling sad. I told myself to be *very* nice to her all night long.

# The Flying Fish

On Monday morning, I led Natalie into our classroom. I had decided I had better take care of her at home *and* at school.

"Hi, everybody," I said.

Hannie and Nancy knew about Natalie's grandfather. I had called them the night before to tell them the news. I guess they had told the other kids already. Everyone was being extra nice to Natalie.

When Natalie took off her coat, Hank hung it up for her.

When Natalie went to her desk, Ricky

jumped up and pulled out her chair.

Addie shared a package of funny stickers with her.

Even Pamela, Jannie, and Leslie were nice to her.

"Do you want some gum, Natalie?" asked Pamela.

"It's assorted flavors," said Jannie. "You can pick first."

"Thanks," said Natalie. She chose a stick of wild cherry.

"I'm going to sharpen my pencils. I can take yours, too," said Leslie.

By the time Ms. Colman came in, everyone had done something to make Natalie feel better. Natalie looked a little confused by the attention. But I think she liked it, too.

"If you need anything, just let me know," I whispered while Ms. Colman was taking attendance.

In the afternoon Mr. Mackey helped us with our kites. They had to be ready by Friday. That was the day of our kite-flying contest.

"Would you please pass the glitter?" asked Addie. She was making a great 3-D star kite, with stars and stripes and glitter on it.

Ricky was making a black bat kite with great big wings. It was spooky.

Hannie was making a kite that looked like a dog. Nancy was making one that looked like a cat.

I was making my flying fish kite. It was very beautiful. It was even more beautiful than the tropical fish kite in Mrs. Moody's store. Here are the colors I put on my kite: red, purple, pink, light blue, yellow, light green.

I looked over at Natalie's kite. It was a diamond shape — sort of. And it was gray. Not a bright and shiny gray. It was gray like a dirty nickel. And the tail was a bunch of torn-up cleaning rags knotted together.

I wondered if Natalie's kite would even fly. Maybe it would be too embarrassed to be seen in the sky.

I wanted to say something nice. I had to think hard.

"Your kite is special, Natalie," I said. "It is not like any of the kites in Mrs. Moody's store." (That was the truth.)

After school, I asked Nancy if she wanted to come over and play.

"It will be you, me, *and* Natalie," I said. I said it loudly enough for Natalie to hear.

I was glad to see that Natalie looked a lot better than she had the night before. Being nice to her was working really well. And you know what? It was easy.

# Tears

Mommy picked Natalie, Nancy, and me up after school. I made sure Natalie sat in the middle. I did not want her to feel left out.

"What would you like for a snack?" I asked when we got home.

"Bread with honey is good," said Natalie. "And apple juice to drink."

"Okay," I replied. "You can have anything you want."

I took out apple juice and three cups. I took out bread and honey for Natalie. I took out crackers, peanut butter, and cheese squeeze for Nancy and me. (It was our favorite snack.)

Nancy and I started spreading peanut butter and cheese on our crackers and eating them. Natalie sat and looked at her bread and honey.

"Is anything wrong?" I asked.

"Um, could you toast the bread?" said Natalie.

"Of course."

I toasted the bread. Then I put it back on Natalie's plate. Natalie still sat and looked at it.

"Is it too dark or something?" I asked.

"It's okay. Could I have some butter?"

I took out butter for Natalie. Nancy and I were already finished with our snack. We had to wait while Natalie spread the butter. We had to wait while she spread the honey. Then we had to wait while she ate. Natalie is a very slow eater.

By the time Natalie finished, we did not have time to play Lovely Ladies or anything fun. We had to do our homework for Ms.

48

Colman. She had given us a worksheet about flying.

When Nancy left, Natalie and I went to my room.

"Do you want to play with Emily Junior?" I asked.

"Ew, no. Rats are gross," said Natalie.

I hoped Emily Junior did not hear her. That would hurt her feelings. I was mad at Natalie for saying something so mean. But I did not tell her so.

Natalie and I had a tea party with Hyacynthia. Then Mommy called, "It's almost time for supper, girls. Please wash up and come downstairs."

I let Natalie wash up first. She left the water dripping and her towel on the floor. But I still did not say a word.

At supper, Natalie took the chicken wing I wanted. She took the biggest piece of cake. And when Seth tried to put honey in his tea, his hands got all sticky. That's because Natalie had dripped honey down the sides of the jar.

After dinner, Andrew did not get to watch his favorite TV show. Natalie wanted to watch another channel.

No one complained. We were all being so, so nice to Natalie.

While she was watching her TV show, the phone rang. I hoped it was for me. But it wasn't.

"Natalie! It's for you," called Mommy. "It's your parents."

"Hi, Mommy. Hi, Daddy," said Natalie into the phone. I could see her chin start to quiver. Two seconds later, she burst into tears.

After the phone call, I tried to cheer Natalie up.

"Do you want me to make you another snack?" I asked.

Natalie shook her head.

"Do you want to wear my new barrette to school tomorrow?"

She shook her head again.

Nothing I tried was working. I was happy when Mommy said it was time for bed.

# The Kite People

On Tuesday afternoon, I invited Nancy and Hannie to my house. I thought that might cheer up Natalie. It did.

"You mean I will get to play with the Three Musketeers?" asked Natalie, with a big smile.

"Yup," I replied. "I have a plan, too."

When we reached my house I told my friends the plan. "I think we should make little paper kites. We can fly them in the yard," I said.

"Great!" Nancy cried. "I will make a kitten kite to go with my cat kite."

"I will make a puppy kite," said Hannie.

"I have an even better idea," said Natalie.

We turned to look at her. Natalie did not usually get ideas.

"Instead of making kites, maybe we can fly ourselves," said Natalie. "There must be a way to do it. We could be kite people."

"I don't know," I said. "Ms. Colman has been teaching us about flying. And she never said anything about people flying by themselves."

"Let's make some wings and try it anyway," said Natalie.

Even though I was worried, I said okay. I did not want Natalie to be unhappy.

We made the wings out of cardboard. We used lots of string to tie the wings to our arms.

"Now let's go outside and try them," said Natalie.

We took turns standing in the middle

of the porch stairs and jumping down. I flapped my wings. But I did not feel as if I were flying. I felt the way I always felt when I jumped from the middle of the stairs.

We tried jumping from the top step next. I flapped my arms hard. Even that did not feel like flying. And when I landed, it hurt my knees.

"Ouch!" I cried.

"I think we need to be higher," said Natalie. "We need more time to flap our wings before we land."

I was getting nervous. Mommy would not be happy if she knew we were jumping from high places. So I thought of a place to try that wasn't *too* high.

"Follow me," I said. I led Nancy, Hannie, and Natalie to the back of the yard shed where we keep our garbage cans. The top of the shed was not much higher than the stairs.

"How will we get to the top?" asked Nancy.

"We will climb on the garbage cans," said Natalie.

We dragged the cans out of the shed. They made an awful lot of noise. Mommy must have heard it. She came running outside just as we were about to climb on the cans.

"What in the world are you girls doing?" cried Mommy. "I cannot *believe* you were thinking of jumping off that roof."

Uh-oh.

"We're sorry, Mrs. Engle," said Hannie.

"You could have hurt yourselves badly," said Mommy. "Karen, I am surprised at you for dreaming up something as dangerous as this. You are old enough to know better."

I looked at Natalie. It had been her idea. Not mine. But I didn't say anything. I did not want to get her into trouble.

"I'm sorry, Mommy," I said. "I should have known better."

Mommy sent Hannie and Nancy home. Then she sent Natalie and me to my room. I did not feel like playing. I did not feel like talking either.

I buried my nose in a book. It was called *Dragonwings* by Laurence Yep. It is about a man who dreams of inventing a flying machine. I wondered if he ever tried flying off a roof. If he did, I bet he got into trouble, too.

# 13

# Karen's Kite

*Glub, glub, glub. Glub, glub, glub.*

It was Wednesday afternoon at school. I was walking around our classroom with my flying fish kite. I was making believe it was swimming through the air. I swam it over to Hannie and Nancy.

"All I have to do now is put on a tail," I said.

"Your kite is gorgeous, Karen," said Hannie. "How do you like mine?"

"It is the best dog kite ever," I told her.

57

There were lots of great kites in the room. Everyone was working hard putting on the finishing touches. We were supposed to have our kites ready by the next afternoon.

I carried my kite back to my seat. Natalie let out a loud sigh.

"I do not know what's wrong with it," she said. She held her kite out in front of her.

I could not find one thing right with it. The kite was lopsided. One corner was ripped. And the rag tail was coming undone. Natalie's kite was a major mess.

But no one told her so. Everyone said nice things to her.

"Cool kite, Natalie," said Ricky.

"Maybe you will win the contest," said Audrey.

"You're finished already," said Hank. "I bet you're the first one."

My classmates were trying to make Natalie feel good. They must have been. Other-

wise they would have said nice things about *my* kite. It was truly spectacular. But no one had said so.

I knew it was not the only great kite in the room, though. Addie's 3-D star kite was perfect. Hank's dragon kite looked almost as good as the one in Mrs. Moody's store. (The one I was going to win.) Even Pamela's butterfly kite was great.

I decided I better say something nice to Natalie, too.

"Your kite is so pretty. I love the color you chose," I said. (It still looked like a dirty nickel to me.)

Then Mr. Mackey looked at my kite carefully. "It is terrific, Karen," he said. "It looks strong. And the colors are so bright. It's going to light up the sky."

"Thank you!" I said.

I was glad Mr. Mackey and Ms. Colman were talking to everyone about their kites, not just to Natalie.

I looked around the room. I wondered

who was going to win the contest. Except for Natalie, everyone had a good chance.

I was so excited. I could hardly wait till Friday. I would get to see my very own kite flying proudly over Stoneybrook Academy.

# Bubbles

"Let's put on bathing suits and take a bubble bath together," said Natalie. "We can fill the tub right up to the top."

Natalie and I were upstairs in my room. Mommy, Seth, and Andrew were downstairs.

I wondered if I should ask Mommy and Seth for permission. After all, Natalie's last idea had gotten me into big trouble. But how much mess could soap and water make?

"Okay," I replied. "You fill the tub. I'll find bathing suits for us."

Filling up the tub would take awhile. I was glad Natalie was in charge of that. It was a boring job.

Now where were my summer clothes? I took out two suitcases and emptied them. No bathing suits there. But I did find my big yellow summer hat. I tried it on.

"How do I look, Goosie?" I asked. Goosie said I looked quite beautiful.

"Why, thank you," I said. I decided to leave my hat out for the next time I played Lovely Ladies.

Then I remembered where Mommy had put my bathing suits. They were in the back of my underwear drawer.

I picked out a red bathing suit and a green striped one. Then I headed for the bathroom.

When I opened the door, I had a big surprise. An enormous tower of bubbles was in the bathtub. Water was sloshing over the side.

"Natalie!" I cried. "The water! Turn off the water!"

Natalie was facing the other way. She was looking at herself in the mirror. Blue cream was smeared all over her face. It was Mommy's special face cream.

"Karen? What's going on up there?" called Mommy.

I hurried to turn off the water. The next thing I knew, Mommy, Seth, and Andrew were standing at the bathroom door.

"Oh, girls! Look what you've done!" cried Mommy.

"Karen made a bubble mess," said Andrew.

"Let's get towels and clean up fast. This water could leak down into the living room," said Seth.

When the floor was dry again, Mommy and Seth came into my room. They wanted to talk about what had happened.

"What is going on, Karen?" said Mommy. "One day you do something dangerous. Then you do something careless."

"This could have cost us a lot of money for no reason," said Seth.

Mommy and Seth were very angry at me. I looked at Natalie. I was waiting for her to tell them it had been her idea. I was waiting for her to tell them she was the one who left the water running. But she didn't. She let me take the blame.

I told Mommy and Seth I was sorry about the flood. When they left, I told Natalie a thing or two.

"It was all your fault and you didn't even say anything!" I shouted.

"Well, you shouldn't have left me there so long," said Natalie.

"I thought I could trust you. But all you know how to do is get me into trouble!"

That did it. Natalie's chin started to quiver. Then she burst into tears. This time I didn't care.

"I would just like to tell you one more thing," I said. "I am not speaking to you anymore."

I turned away from Natalie. I did not say another word all night.

# Meanie Karen

When I woke up on Thursday, I made a big mistake. I said, "Hi, Natalie." I forgot I was not talking to her.

I did not say another word until breakfast. Then Seth asked for the butter. It was on the other side of Natalie. So I had to say, "Butter, please."

I had said four words since our fight. But I would not say anything else to Natalie if I could help it.

When we arrived at school, I put down

my pack. Then I went to visit Hannie and Nancy. I left Natalie by herself.

"Why don't you ask Natalie to come sit with us?" asked Hannie.

"I am not talking to Natalie," I announced. "We had a fight."

A few kids at the back of the room heard me. They gave me crabby looks.

"What happened?" asked Hannie.

I did not have a chance to answer because Ms. Colman came in.

"Good morning, everyone," she said. "Please take your seats."

While Ms. Colman was taking attendance, I heard some kids whispering about me. They were calling me "Meanie Karen," because I was not talking to Natalie.

I wished lunchtime would come fast. I would tell everyone what Natalie had done. Then they would understand why I was not talking to her.

When we were seated in the cafeteria, I made an announcement, "I am going to tell what happened, in case anyone is interested."

I told everyone how Natalie let the water run over the bathtub. I told them how she let me take the blame.

When I finished, Nancy and Hannie pulled me aside.

"Her *grand*father *died*," said Hannie. "You have to be *nice* to her."

"I am sorry about Natalie's grandfather," I said. "But she was the one being mean, not me."

The rest of the kids gathered around Natalie. I could not believe they were taking her side. Natalie looked in my direction. She thought she was so great just because everyone was mad at me.

Back in our classroom, Ms. Colman and Mr. Mackey helped us put the finishing touches on our kites. The afternoon was supposed to be fun. But it wasn't. I was not talking to Natalie. And now the other kids were not talking to me.

I was in a bad, bad mood. I knocked over Natalie's box of crayons accidentally on purpose. I did not say I was sorry. First of all, I was not sorry one bit. Second of all, if I said I was sorry I would have been talking to her. And I did not want to talk to Natalie Springer ever again.

"Your kite looks like it's finished, Karen. All you have to do now is attach the line," said Mr. Mackey. "I'll show you how."

I did a very good job attaching the line. My kite was ready for the contest.

I thought that would make me happy. But it didn't. Boo.

16

# The Sleepover

"Good morning, Goosie. Good morning, Emily Junior. Good morning, Hyacynthia."

I said good morning to every doll and toy in my room. I did *not* say good morning to Natalie.

It was Friday. It was the day of the kite-flying contest and the sleepover. No way was I going to be in a bad mood. After all, how many chances would I get to have a sleepover in my wonderful school with my wonderful teachers?

I put my pajamas in my pack and rolled up my sleeping bag.

"I'll see you tomorrow," I said to my dolls. "I'm sleeping over at school."

The next day would be Saturday. Then it would be Sunday. On Sunday, Natalie's parents were coming home. Thank goodness.

That day my friends and I had a hard time concentrating. We could hardly wait for school to end and the contest to begin.

I kept turning around to look at Hannie and Nancy and pointing to the clock on the wall. (They thought I was being a meanie to Natalie, but at least they were still talking to me.)

At the end of the day, Mr. Mackey came to our room with three parents who were going to help at the sleepover.

"Is everyone ready?" he asked.

"Ready!" we answered.

"All right, then," said Mr. Mackey. "We have beautiful weather for our contest. The sky is clear and there's a nice breeze. I think you know how the contest is going to work, but I will let Ms. Colman explain it to you one more time, so there won't be any confusion. Ms. Colman?"

"Class, in just a little while, we will go outside to launch our kites. You will get to watch them fly for awhile. Then we will come back inside, play some games, eat dinner, and have our sleepover. The adults will take turns watching the kites. We will keep a record of the time that each one comes down. Whoever owns the last kite to come down will win Mrs. Moody's gift certificate. Are there any questions?"

No one had a question.

"Then it is time to line up," said Mr. Mackey. "The contest is about to begin."

As we left the room, I whispered to my beautiful flying fish, "Do you think we can win?"

*Glub, glub.* (She said she would try her best.)

I *really* wanted to win the prize. But I knew it would not be easy. So many great kites were in the room.

I closed my eyes. Then I crossed my arms and my fingers and my toes.

"Please, please, please let me win," I wished.

The next thing I knew, I was out in the sunshine with the breeze on my face.

# The Kite Fight

"Everyone spread out across the playground, please," called Ms. Colman.

Ms. Colman told us that the playground was a good place for kite flying. There were no trees or wires for our kites to get caught in.

"This is what to do," said Mr. Mackey. He told us to stand with our backs to the wind. That way the wind could do its work. It would carry our kites up in the air.

"Hold up your kites. When I say go, let go of your kite and unwind the line."

I held out my kite. I hopped from one foot to the other. That was not part of Mr. Mackey's instructions. But I could hardly wait for Mr. Mackey to call . . .

"Go!"

I let go of my kite and unwound the line the way I was supposed to. My flying fish sailed up, up, up into the sky.

"Good-bye, Fish! Have a nice flight. Don't come back too soon!" I called.

"Bat kite, please be a winner!" called Ricky.

All around me kites were sailing into the sky. A few kids were having trouble. They were either facing the wrong way, or letting out the line too quickly.

Natalie was doing everything right. But she was still having trouble. That was because her kite was such a mess.

Ms. Colman, Mr. Mackey, and the parents helped out. Soon all the kites — even Natalie's — were in the air.

We attached our lines to hooks in the ground. Then we stood back and watched.

It was so, so beautiful. Eighteen kites were flying high. I waved to my fish.

Suddenly the wind blew harder. My line jerked. My kite took a nose dive. Everyone watched my kite crash into Natalie's. For a few seconds, the two kites looked as if they were fighting with each other.

Natalie's kite did not have a chance. It zoomed to the ground. Then the wind died down and my kite sailed back up where it had started.

I took one look at Natalie and she burst into tears.

"You broke my kite!" she cried.

I did not say a word. I was still not talking to Natalie. Anyway, I did not think I had to explain. Everyone saw what had happened. The wind started the kite fight. Not me. I was not even holding the line.

I was angry at Natalie for getting me into trouble before. But I was sorry for her too because her grandfather died. And because now her kite had fallen down.

My feelings were all mixed up.

# Sleeping at School

"You didn't do anything wrong," said Hannie.

"That's right," said Nancy. "It was not your fault."

The Three Musketeers were standing in a group on the playground. Everyone else was gathered around Natalie again.

Pamela stomped over to me. "How could you do that, Karen Brewer?" she said. "How could you knock Natalie's kite out of the sky?"

"That is ridiculous!" I said. "I did not

touch Natalie's kite and you know it."

Big-mouth Bobby came over next. "It's bad enough you would not talk to Natalie. You did not have to make her lose the contest, too," he said.

I stuck my tongue out at him.

"Come on, let's go sit on the swings. We can watch our kites from there," said Nancy.

My classmates and I watched the kites for awhile. When we were tired of watching them we went inside. Most of the kids had forgotten about the kite fight by the time we got there. I was glad. I wanted to have fun at the sleepover.

Natalie was still mad at me, though. I felt sorry for her. I really did. But I decided the best thing to do was ignore her.

Our sleepover was in the gym. That was fun because we could run around a lot.

"Do you want to play dodge ball, or jump rope?" Hannie asked Nancy and me.

I was trying to decide when Ms. Colman

called, "Will someone help me put this chart up on the wall?"

"I will!" I said. I love to help Ms. Colman — especially with important jobs.

At the top of the chart were big letters that said KITE-FLYING CONTEST. Underneath were two columns. One said, "Name of Student." The other said, "Kite-Flying Time."

The first line was already filled in. It said: *Natalie Springer. Fifteen minutes.*

I would hate to be the first one on the chart. I hoped I would be the last one. Then I would be the winner.

I was on my way to the jump rope corner when Mr. Mackey called, "Kite down!"

Bobby Gianelli's name went up on the chart. His kite-flying time was forty-five minutes.

"Too bad," said Ricky. "It was a neat kite."

I was having a lot of fun at the party. So were most of the other kids. Every once in awhile, one of the grown-ups called, "Kite

down!" Then we'd run to the chart to see whose name and time had gone up.

By the time we had eaten our dinner, six kites had come down.

By the time we went to sleep, ten kites had come down.

"Fly, fish kite, fly!" I whispered as I closed my eyes. I hoped my kite would fly all through the night.

# The Winner

"Rise and shine, everyone," said Ms. Colman on Saturday morning. "Only two kites are still flying. They belong to Karen and Hank."

"Yes!" I cried. I tumbled out of my sleeping bag. I ran to the window. There they were — Hank's dragon kite and my flying fish kite.

We took turns going to the bathroom. Then we lined up to go to the cafeteria for breakfast. We were on our way out of the gym when Mr. Mackey called, "Kite down!"

We looked outside. My flying fish kite was the only kite left in the sky.

"Congratulations, Karen. You have won the contest," said Mr. Mackey.

I could not believe it. There had been so many great kites. I wanted to be the winner, but I had not really and truly thought it would happen.

"You won, Karen, you won!" cried Hannie.

"I am really happy for you," said Nancy.

"Thanks!" I replied.

I was so excited I could hardly eat any breakfast. I tried to wait patiently for it to end. Finally my friends and I returned to our classroom to meet our parents. Mrs. Moody was there waiting for us, too.

"Congratulations to everyone. Your kites were terrific," she said. "And now I would like to present the gift certificate to our winner, Karen Brewer. Karen, will you please come here?"

I walked to the front of the room. (I did not have very far to go since I sit in the first row.) Mrs. Moody handed me my prize.

I took the certificate in one hand. I shook Mrs. Moody's hand with the other. I faced my class and smiled a great big smile.

"Thank you, Mrs. Moody," I said. Then I made an announcement. "I would like to share my prize with Natalie Springer. The kite fight yesterday was not fair. If the wind had not made my kite hit Natalie's, maybe Natalie's kite would have stayed up a long time. Maybe she would have won the contest."

I did not really believe that Natalie's kite could have won the contest. But I felt bad for Natalie. She had had a hard week. First she had lost her grandfather. Then we had had our fight. I thought about the fight. She should not have let me take the blame for everything by myself. But I had made a mistake, too. I should have told my mother the truth. That would have been better than giving Natalie the silent treatment.

For the first time in days, Natalie smiled at me. I was glad I had decided to share my prize with her. So were the other kids. They were clapping for me and for Natalie.

"Congratulations, Natalie," I said.

"Thanks, Karen," she replied.

We held up the gift certificate together, so everyone could see it.

# The Wonderful Kite

My classmates were packing their things and rolling up their kites. Not much was left of Natalie's kite. But she put a few pieces of it in her bag anyway.

Natalie and I looked at each other. At the exact same moment we both said, "I'm sorry."

Then I said, "I shouldn't have stopped talking to you."

And Natalie said, "I shouldn't have let you take the blame for everything."

You know what she said next?

"You should keep the gift certificate, Karen. I did not win it. You did."

I thought about keeping it, but that was not what I really wanted to do.

"It's okay," I said. "I *want* to split it with you."

"I am going to tell your mother the truth about the bathtub," said Natalie.

She was? Maybe Natalie would tell my mother *everything*.

"Will you tell her it was your idea for us to be kite people, too?" I asked.

"Okay," agreed Natalie. "I will tell her that, too."

I was glad Natalie and I had made up. We would never be best friends. But fighting was no fun.

I even missed Natalie a little after she went home on Sunday. On Wednesday afternoon, Natalie called me at the little house to tell me she had used her half of the gift certificate.

"I got a caterpillar kite," she said. "It's really pretty."

I wished I had my new dragon kite. I would have to think of a way to earn the money I needed to buy it. Maybe I could start a pet-washing business. I would start with Midgie. I could charge twenty or thirty dollars a bath. (Just kidding.)

"Hey, Karen?" said Andrew. He was standing outside my room. "It's a windy day. Could you come fly your fish kite with me?"

"I'm busy, Andrew," I replied.

"You don't look busy," said Andrew.

"I may not look it. But I am. I am thinking," I explained. Little brothers do not always understand these things.

"But, look, it's windy," said Andrew again.

I looked out the window. It really was the perfect day for flying my kite.

"Oh, all right," I said. "Let's go."

I carried the kite. I let Andrew walk behind me carrying the line.

When we were standing in the backyard, I launched my kite. As soon as it was in the air, Andrew started laughing and shouting and jumping up and down.

"I want to fly a kite, too!" he said. "This is so much fun!"

That gave me an idea. I already had a wonderful kite. Mine. My flying fish kite. I really did not need another one. I pulled my fish kite in.

I was going to use my prize to buy a kite for Andrew. Then we could fly our kites together.

"Come on, Andrew," I said. "Let's see if Mommy can drive us to Mrs. Moody's Kite Store."

## About the Author

ANN M. MARTIN lives in New York City and loves animals, especially cats. She has two cats of her own, Mouse and Rosie.

Other books by Ann M. Martin that you might enjoy are *Stage Fright*; *Me and Katie (the Pest)*; and the books in *The Baby-sitters Club* series.

Ann likes ice cream and *I Love Lucy*. And she has her own little sister, whose name is Jane.

## Little Sister

Don't miss #48

## KAREN'S TWO FAMILIES

I noticed that Nancy was frowning at me. "What do you mean you hate being a two-two?" she asked. "I thought you liked it."

"I used to," I admitted. "But lately I feel like I miss out on *every*thing at the big house. I did not know Emily was big enough for a big-girl bed. I did not know about Nannie's bowling team. I do not even know Kristy's friends now. Plus, I miss Daddy all the time. I miss everyone. The pets, too. I am only at the big house four days each month, you know. That is not much time at all. It is hardly anything."

"Boy," said Hannie. "I used to wish I could be a two-two like you."

I sighed. "I guess it is not *all* bad," I said after awhile.

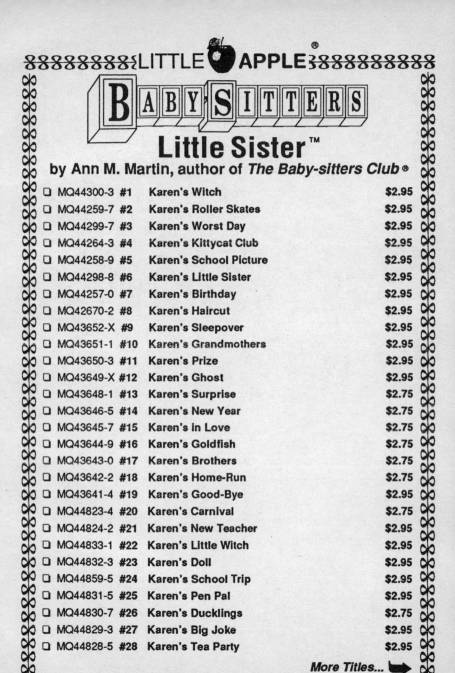

# LITTLE APPLE®

# BABY-SITTERS

## Little Sister™

### by Ann M. Martin, author of *The Baby-sitters Club* ®

| | | | |
|---|---|---|---|
| ❑ | MQ44300-3 | #1  | Karen's Witch | $2.95 |
| ❑ | MQ44259-7 | #2  | Karen's Roller Skates | $2.95 |
| ❑ | MQ44299-7 | #3  | Karen's Worst Day | $2.95 |
| ❑ | MQ44264-3 | #4  | Karen's Kittycat Club | $2.95 |
| ❑ | MQ44258-9 | #5  | Karen's School Picture | $2.95 |
| ❑ | MQ44298-8 | #6  | Karen's Little Sister | $2.95 |
| ❑ | MQ44257-0 | #7  | Karen's Birthday | $2.95 |
| ❑ | MQ42670-2 | #8  | Karen's Haircut | $2.95 |
| ❑ | MQ43652-X | #9  | Karen's Sleepover | $2.95 |
| ❑ | MQ43651-1 | #10 | Karen's Grandmothers | $2.95 |
| ❑ | MQ43650-3 | #11 | Karen's Prize | $2.95 |
| ❑ | MQ43649-X | #12 | Karen's Ghost | $2.95 |
| ❑ | MQ43648-1 | #13 | Karen's Surprise | $2.75 |
| ❑ | MQ43646-5 | #14 | Karen's New Year | $2.75 |
| ❑ | MQ43645-7 | #15 | Karen's in Love | $2.75 |
| ❑ | MQ43644-9 | #16 | Karen's Goldfish | $2.75 |
| ❑ | MQ43643-0 | #17 | Karen's Brothers | $2.75 |
| ❑ | MQ43642-2 | #18 | Karen's Home-Run | $2.75 |
| ❑ | MQ43641-4 | #19 | Karen's Good-Bye | $2.95 |
| ❑ | MQ44823-4 | #20 | Karen's Carnival | $2.75 |
| ❑ | MQ44824-2 | #21 | Karen's New Teacher | $2.95 |
| ❑ | MQ44833-1 | #22 | Karen's Little Witch | $2.95 |
| ❑ | MQ44832-3 | #23 | Karen's Doll | $2.95 |
| ❑ | MQ44859-5 | #24 | Karen's School Trip | $2.95 |
| ❑ | MQ44831-5 | #25 | Karen's Pen Pal | $2.95 |
| ❑ | MQ44830-7 | #26 | Karen's Ducklings | $2.75 |
| ❑ | MQ44829-3 | #27 | Karen's Big Joke | $2.95 |
| ❑ | MQ44828-5 | #28 | Karen's Tea Party | $2.95 |

*More Titles...* ➡

*The Baby-sitters Little Sister titles continued...*

| | | | |
|---|---|---|---|
| ❑ | MQ44825-0 #29 | Karen's Cartwheel | $2.75 |
| ❑ | MQ45645-8 #30 | Karen's Kittens | $2.75 |
| ❑ | MQ45646-6 #31 | Karen's Bully | $2.95 |
| ❑ | MQ45647-4 #32 | Karen's Pumpkin Patch | $2.95 |
| ❑ | MQ45648-2 #33 | Karen's Secret | $2.95 |
| ❑ | MQ45650-4 #34 | Karen's Snow Day | $2.95 |
| ❑ | MQ45652-0 #35 | Karen's Doll Hospital | $2.95 |
| ❑ | MQ45651-2 #36 | Karen's New Friend | $2.95 |
| ❑ | MQ45653-9 #37 | Karen's Tuba | $2.95 |
| ❑ | MQ45655-5 #38 | Karen's Big Lie | $2.95 |
| ❑ | MQ45654-7 #39 | Karen's Wedding | $2.95 |
| ❑ | MQ47040-X #40 | Karen's Newspaper | $2.95 |
| ❑ | MQ47041-8 #41 | Karen's School | $2.95 |
| ❑ | MQ47042-6 #42 | Karen's Pizza Party | $2.95 |
| ❑ | MQ46912-6 #43 | Karen's Toothache | $2.95 |
| ❑ | MQ47043-4 #44 | Karen's Big Weekend | $2.95 |
| ❑ | MQ47044-2 #45 | Karen's Twin | $2.95 |
| ❑ | MQ47045-0 #46 | Karen's Baby-sitter | $2.95 |
| ❑ | MQ43647-3 | Karen's Wish   Super Special #1 | $2.95 |
| ❑ | MQ44834-X | Karen's Plane Trip   Super Special #2 | $3.25 |
| ❑ | MQ44827-7 | Karen's Mystery   Super Special #3 | $2.95 |
| ❑ | MQ45644-X | Karen's Three Musketeers   Super Special #4 | $2.95 |
| ❑ | MQ45649-0 | Karen's Baby   Super Special #5 | $3.25 |
| ❑ | MQ46911-8 | Karen's Campout   Super Special #6 | $3.25 |

**Available wherever you buy books, or use this order form.**

- - - - - - - - - - - - - - - - - - - - - - - - - - - - - - - - - - - -

**Scholastic Inc., P.O. Box 7502, 2931 E. McCarty Street, Jefferson City, MO 65102**

Please send me the books I have checked above. I am enclosing $ _____ (please add $2.00 to cover shipping and handling). Send check or money order - no cash or C.O.Ds please.

Name _____ Birthdate _____

Address _____

City _____ State/Zip _____

Please allow four to six weeks for delivery. Offer good in U.S.A. only. Sorry, mail orders are not available to residents to Canada. Prices subject to change.                      BLS793

**APPLE®** PAPERBACKS

## More books you will love by...

# ANN M. MARTIN
### author of your favorite series

## Don't miss any of these
## great Apple ® Paperbacks

| | | |
|---|---|---|
| ❏ MW43622-8 | **Bummer Summer** | **$2.95** |
| ❏ MW43621-X | **Inside Out** | **$2.95** |
| ❏ MW43828-X | **Ma and Pa Dracula** | **$2.95** |
| ❏ MW43618-X | **Me and Katie (the Pest)** | **$2.95** |
| ❏ MW43619-8 | **Stage Fright** | **$2.75** |
| ❏ MW43620-1 | **Ten Kids, No Pets** | **$2.75** |
| ❏ MW43625-2 | **With You and Without You** | **$2.95** |
| ❏ MW42809-8 | **Yours Turly, Shirley** | **$2.95** |

### Available wherever you buy books...
### or use this order form.

Scholastic Inc., P.O. Box 7502, 2931 East McCarty Street, Jefferson City, MO 65102

Please send me the books I have checked above. I am enclosing $———— (please add
$2.00 to cover shipping and handling). Send check or money order — no cash or
C.O.D.s please.

Name ——————————————————————————————————————————

Address ————————————————————————————————————————

City————————————————————————— State/Zip ——————————————

Please allow four to six weeks for delivery. Offer good in the U.S. only. Sorry, mail orders are not available to
residents of Canada. Prices subject to change.

AM991